Dog Breath

To Dan — CB

To Max and his doggy breath. You're the best brother a gal could have. — BK

Text copyright © 2011 Carolyn Beck
Illustrations copyright © 2011 Brooke Kerrigan

Published in Canada by Fitzhenry & Whiteside, 195 Allstate Parkway, Markham, Ontario L3R 4T8

Published in the United States by Fitzhenry & Whiteside, 311 Washington Street, Brighton, Massachusetts 02135

www.fitzhenry.ca   godwit@fitzhenry.ca

10 9 8 7 6 5 4 3 2 1

Library and Archives Canada Cataloguing in Publication
Beck, Carolyn
     Dog breath / Carolyn Beck ; illustrated by Brooke Kerrigan.
ISBN 978-1-55455-180-4
     I. Kerrigan, Brooke II. Title.
PS8553.E2949D64 2011   jC813'.6   C2011-904348-3

Publisher Cataloging-in-Publication Data (U.S)
Beck, Carolyn.
     Dog Breath / Carolyn Beck ; Brooke Kerrigan.
[32] p. : col. ill. ; cm.
ISBN: 978-1-55455-180-4
1. Dogs – Juvenile literature. I. Kerrigan, Brooke. II. Title.
[E] dc22   PZ7.B7665Ta   2011

Fitzhenry & Whiteside acknowledges with thanks the Canada Council for the Arts, and the Ontario Arts Council for their support of our publishing program. We acknowledge the financial support of the Government of Canada through the Canada Book Fund (CBF) for our publishing activities.

Canada Council   Conseil des Arts
for the Arts   du Canada

ONTARIO ARTS COUNCIL
CONSEIL DES ARTS DE L'ONTARIO

Cover and interior design by Blair Kerrigan/Glyphics
Cover image by Brooke Kerrigan
Printed in Canada

Fitzhenry & Whiteside
www.fitzhenry.ca

Prrrr...

Dog Breath

Carolyn Beck • Illustrated by Brooke Kerrigan

Your favourite bone sits
on the edge of the rug
at the foot of my bed
in that spot where the sun
makes a big, warm puddle
in the middle of the afternoon.

Just the way you left it.

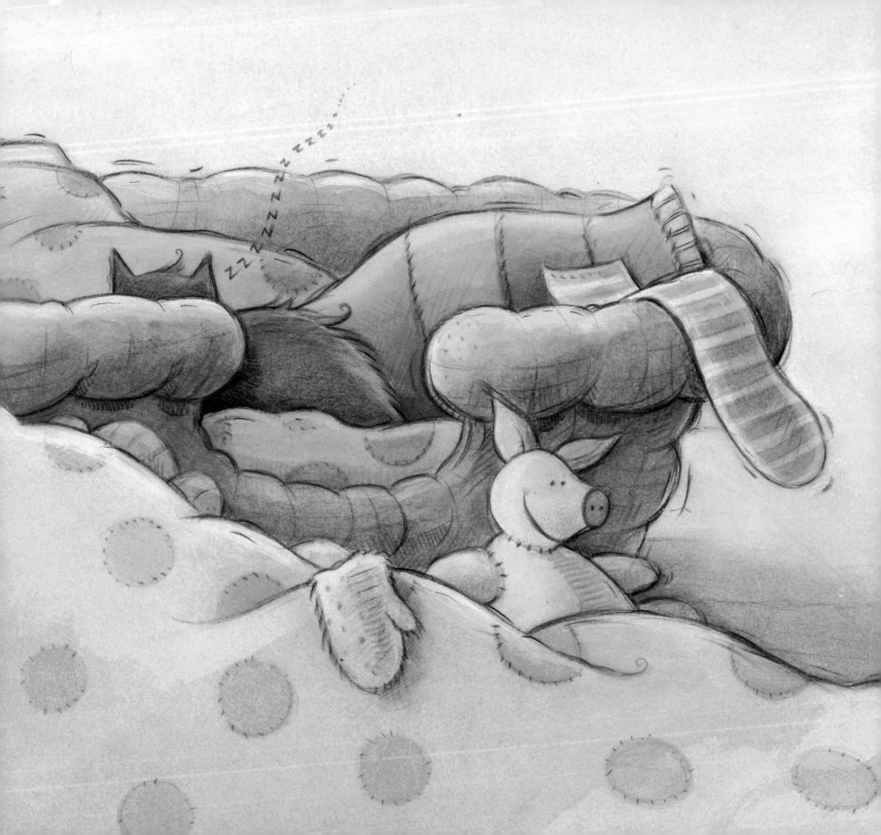

Two floorboards over
in the lumpy shadow of your basket
lie your red rubber ball,
ragged with toothmarks,

and a stolen sock, no toe left.

We slept here
every night—
you in your basket,
curled nose to tail
on your dug-bare cushion,
me in my bed,
tucked into my quilt.
Sometimes you twitched and
woofed inside a dream.
Squirrels.

Sometimes
I woke
not knowing
what was real
till your nose
touched my face.

Dog breath.

What is real
is the curtain
ruffling at the window,
pulling away
from the quiet in here,
slipping
outside
where the wind
runs through the trees
like a happy dog—
free.

You escaped any chance you got.
If the door opened a crack,
if for one second we forgot
how crafty you were,
out you went—
raiding garbage cans,
finding stinks to roll in,

following your nose
for hours and hours
while we called
and called,
thinking the worst.

The worst.

Suddenly, there you were
at the door,
scratching to come in,
smelling like rotten cheese,
looking all waggy and happy with yourself.
At first
all we did was cry some more.
Tears of lost
turned to tears of found.

Then we hauled you to the tub.
Wet and skinny,
fur stuck to your bones,
you looked pretty sorry for yourself
till you shook end to end.
Revenge!

We all ran for cover,
laughing our heads off.

You howled your head off
every time I played my clarinet.

And dribbled
your long, cool toilet drinks
halfway through the house.

That wound-up tail of yours
swept good china cups
right off the coffee table.
Tea islands
all over the couch,
the carpet,
and once,
Great-Grandmother's
white
silk
suit.

You chewed the mail.

And ate my dinner
on liver night
so quietly not even the liver
knew.

You stole socks.
Shoes. Boots.
Gloves and mittens.
Only ones
never pairs.

And food—
anything
you could get your
chops on.

Once, you stole a whole turkey
and the bowl of Brussels sprouts beside it:
a special dinner for guests, with good clothes
and *best manners*.
I guess you didn't know.
Mom called you a wretched thief
and said, "It'll have to be hamburgers."
You snatched one of those, too,
right off
crotchety Isabel Grimpley's lap
and got me in trouble
for snickering.

You were trouble all right.

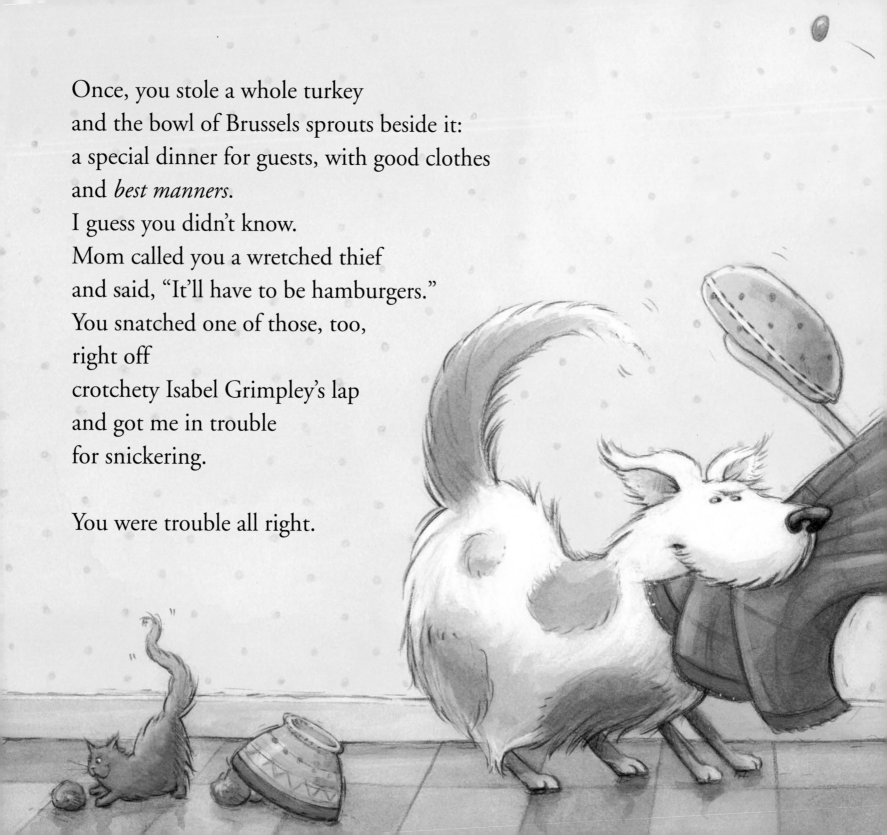

Last week you really did it:
you ate my birthday cake—
the whole thing,
candles, too—
and got yourself so stuffed
you threw it up.

I was so mad I yelled,
"I hate you!"
not knowing
you'd never steal
another birthday cake.

Even now
I still remember
to push a cake
way back
from the edge of the counter
so your big pink tongue
doesn't get a swipe.

I check for
hairs
on my toothbrush.

And dribbles
on the toilet seat.

I tiptoe in the front door,
listening for your claws
clicking across the floor,
the *ji-ji-jing-jing* of your collar,
thinking for a second
that you'll come slobbering at me—
tail whipping,
nose sliming my glasses,
your stinky,
garbage-eating,
toilet-drinking,
dog breath
hot on my face,
the worst dog breath
in the whole universe.

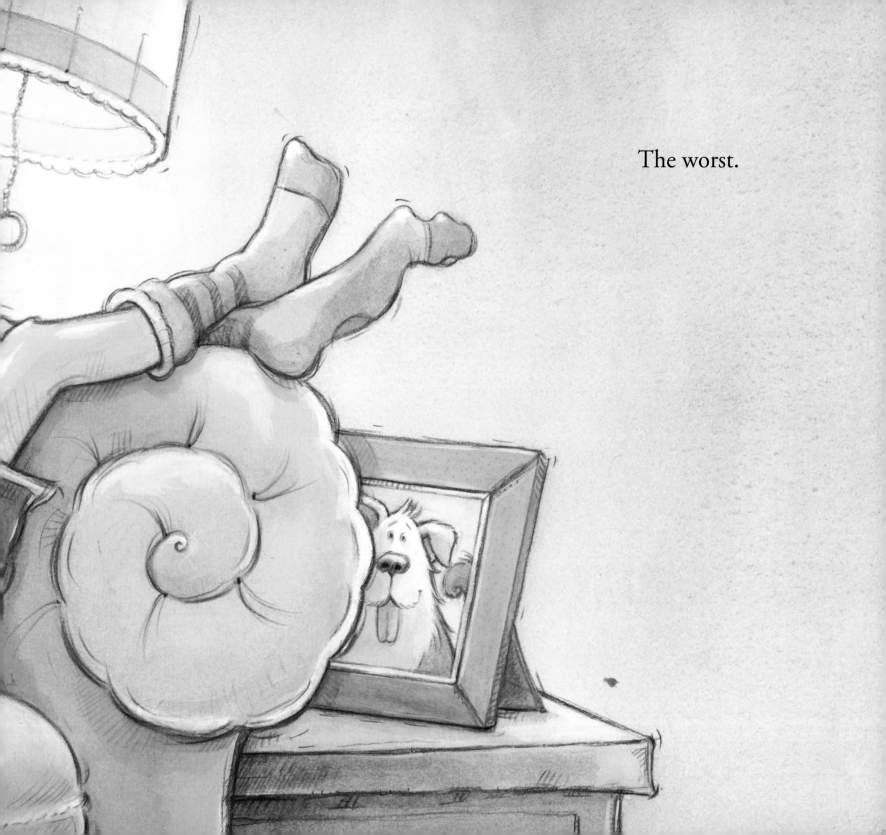

The worst.